For Elias
With thanks to Jerry & Ron
L.K.

For Salvador & Hazel
S.P.

Based on the quote:

"It's not what you look at that matters, it's what you see"

Henry David Thoreau

First Published 2017 by Tiny Tree Children's Books
(an imprint of Matthew James Publishing Ltd)
Unit 46 Goyt Mill
Upper Hibbert Lane
Marple SK6 7HX, UK
www.matthewjamespublishing.com
ISBN: 978-1-910265-44-4

Illustrations by Steffie Padmos
Typesetting by Roel de Jonge
Front and back endpaper design by Dimphy Padmos
Printed in the UK by Chapel Print LTD
Distribution for The Netherlands and Belgium
by sirqls Publishing. www.sirqls.eu

Lilian Kars &
Steffie Padmos

Ilias' Mountain

Chapter one
ILIAS

If you are thinking of writing a story, it probably wouldn't be about a boy like Ilias.

Ilias was a very normal boy, with plain brown, curly hair. His teeth were a bit crooked and his nose a little too big. But what people always did notice, were his eyes. Ilias looked at the world through the most beautiful brown, gold sparkling eyes. Other than that, he was a normal child. Not too tall and not too small, just an ordinary boy. But sometimes the most ordinary kids do extraordinary things.

The village where Ilias lived was just as ordinary as he was. All the houses were white - or used to be - and all had big wooden doors. Only the important people were allowed to paint their doors red, so most of the doors stayed brown. In the middle of the village you could see a big square with a fountain. During summer it spurted water over the four little angels who held each other's hands.

If you looked closely, you could see how the water had carved
little grooves into their wings.

Every winter Ilias put his fingers in the grooves to see how
much had been washed away. When he was little, he once told
his mum how scared he was that one day the angels wouldn't
be able to fly anymore. His mum laughed and told him not to
say such silly things. Of course Ilias didn't want to be silly,
so he never mentioned it again. And he made sure nobody saw
him checking the wings every year.

As in any normal village the church, with tower and big bell, and the pub were found in the square. The pub was called THE BRAVE HUNTSMAN, though the owner never hunted.

All the meat he served, he bought at MR MOONEY'S MARVELOUS MEAT, the butcher next door. Next to MR MOONEY'S was a greengrocer, and a little flower shop where the bakery used to be.

A couple of years ago, Thomas Bradley, from
BRADLEY'S BREAD, PIES AND PASTRIES,
moved to the edge of the village. Like any
baker, he always quietly baked his bread in
the middle of the night, but suddenly
he started to sing out or whistle!
And though the villagers loved him,

his wife and especially his bread, they didn't
care much for this midnight entertainment.
Thomas needed more space, and the villagers
more sleep. So after a good talk at
THE BRAVE HUNTSMAN, Thomas moved,
whistling.

A little stream meandered right through the village. In spring it pretended to be a wild river, carrying down big rocks from the surrounding mountains. During summer Ilias and his friends used these rocks to build dams, so they could paddle around in a still bit of water. Or they hopped from one rock to another to cross over, so they wouldn't need the old, wooden bridge.

There was just one road to enter or leave the village. You only used it if it was really, really necessary to go beyond the mountains, and Ilias never had thought it was. Neither did his parents or any of the kids from school.

The house where Ilias lived stood right in
the center of the village, by the square with
the fountain. It was a big house with large
windows and shining steps.

Next to the deep red painted door was a
big bell which you could hear throughout
the whole house. The bell was heard often,
because Ilias' father was a doctor; the
only doctor around. That made him a very
important man and made Ilias very proud.
His father seemed to like it less; a lot less.
But then again, his father did not like much.

That was very obvious the night this story actually begins. Ilias sensed it as soon as he entered the room. The air felt so much heavier than in the hallway, maybe that's why his father was resting his head in his hands. Mum winked at him, not a very happy wink, more the warning kind.

His father sighed. "Oh well," he said, "it is what it is. And it will never change, will it?"

Mum didn't answer, and neither did Ilias. He learned a long time ago that it was better not to say anything when Dad looked like he did now.

His little sister Ella obviously had not learned that yet. Or maybe she just wanted things to be different today. She burst into the room and threw her bag on the table. "I was top of the class, I was top of the class." She danced around her father and tried to put her small arms around his neck. But father jumped up, wiped her bag from the table and yelled: "When will I ever have some peace and quiet in my own home?!"

He left the room with big, angry steps.
One minute later Ilias heard the deep red
door slam behind him. Through the window
he watched his father cross the square, on his
way to the mountain. Mum would be busy for
a while with Emma's tears as well as her own,
so Ilias quietly went up to his room.
His stomach hurt, and his legs felt like
chewing gum, but somehow they carried
him upstairs.

Ilias thought he had the best room in the
whole house, although it was the smallest.
It fitted his desk, wardrobe, a chair and
his bed. Not much, but enough. And in the
sloping roof, right above his bed, was a
window.

When he sat on his bed he could overlook
half of the village, the whole square and a
big part of the river. When he lay down, he
just saw the top of a mountain and the sky.
Not just any mountain, but the one that really
mattered to him: their mountain. Not that
they owned it of course, but it was the one
where Mum and Dad collected and carried
up their stones.

Ilias let out a deep sigh. His dad would probably stay away all night: it looked like he had a lot of carrying to do. At least the moon was bright so Dad would see properly.

His heart felt heavy and so did his eyes. Although many questions and worries were running around in his head, he knew he had to go to sleep. Tomorrow he would go and talk to the baker. The baker would find the time. No matter how many loaves of bread or pies he needed to bake, there always seemed to be enough time to talk to him.

Ilias set his alarm at 4.45 AM. It was early, but the best time to have an undisturbed talk. Then he slowly fell asleep, dreaming of big rocks and angels with broken wings.

Chapter two
THE BAKER

The next morning Ilias snuck down the stairs. He was careful not to bump into his father who just got home. As he tiptoed to the backdoor he could hear him flush the toilet. As quickly as he could, Ilias opened the creaking door and grabbed his bike. And before the bell in the tower had struck five, he had already crossed the square.

He raced through the small streets, passed his grandparents' house, went right across the wooden bridge and then made a left turn. He knew it would only be a couple more minutes before he would hear the baker sing. Just as the first 'ladidaaah' reached his ears, he saw a little sunbeam shine upon their mountain. He felt his eyes tear up and quickly wiped them with his sleeve.

"Hey Brownie, what are you doing here so early?" The baker slapped Ilias on his shoulder and pretended not to see the redness of his eyes. When they first met the baker had said that Ilias' eyes reminded him of his beautiful fresh brownies and had called him 'Brownie'. Ilias loved brownies, and the baker, ever since.

"Come on, don't just stand there, move that bag of flour!" For more than an hour Ilias was dragging and stacking, kneading and eating. The baker never put anything in his store that had not been tasted by them first.

"Like with all things in life, you have to keep in charge of the flavor." he always said.

When all the bread was in the oven, the pastries
were waiting to be finished with whipped cream
and the bucket next to the door was filled with
fresh French bread, it was finally time for a coffee,
and the talk. For the first time this year it was
warm enough to sit outside, on the river bank.
Ilias got a cup of tea; the baker thought he was
too young for coffee.

"My father went up the mountain again last night." There, he finally said it.

"Hmm, that's about the fourth time this month, isn't it?" the baker asked, while dipping a piece of warm, fresh bread into his coffee.

"Yep, the fourth time." Ilias tried to make his voice sound as steady as possible. Stupid tears... He quickly took a sip of his tea. "And later my Mum will probably go as well, as soon as she has dropped Ella off at Grandma's."

That came out really wobbly and Ilias looked at the mountain which now bathed in the morning sun.

"I hate that mountain!" he yelled and was shocked by his outburst. The baker did not seem very impressed. He just took another bite from his bread, chewed a while and then calmly said, "No, you don't."

He gently put down his coffee and continued: "Sometimes we just have stones to carry, it's always been like that and that's how it will always be."

"You sound just like my father!" He knew he was yelling again but Ilias just couldn't help himself. "Why?? What's the point?"

"Have you ever been up there?" Ilias shook his head and mumbled "Next week". Mum or Dad had never wanted to take him up. But next week he turned twelve, so he could go by himself. Maybe then he would understand.

"Will you be going alone?" the baker asked, while he seemed very interested in a small ladybug on his shoe. Ilias thought for a while. Like every child in the village, a pile of stones was waiting there for him to carry up.

He had a big pile, so he could use some help. He didn't know the path and from the few things his dad had told him, he knew it would be hard. But, like his father always said, everybody had to carry his own load. "Yes," Ilias tried to sound as brave as he wanted to be, "I will go alone".

The baker nodded, carefully picked up the ladybug and placed it on a daisy. Then he got up and brushed some breadcrumbs from his apron with his hands. "If you change your mind, I will go with you, Brownie", he said, just before he went back in again. Ilias loved the baker.

Chapter three
GOING UP THE MOUNTAIN

That Thursday Ilias turned twelve. Friday
after school he took his bike and rode to the
mountain. He felt sick, but told himself he
had eaten too much cake yesterday. It was
a beautiful cake, a present from the baker
of course. Everybody loved it, Grandpa and
Grandma, Ella, Mum, even Dad had a piece!
It felt like a real party but then Luke, his best
friend, had to spoil it all by asking him when
he would go up the mountain. Everybody
suddenly stopped talking. They all knew
about the big pile of rocks Ilias had collected
over the last couple of years. Fortunately,
at that moment Ella dropped her cake.

When Ilias reached his mountain and his rocks he had no idea what to do. He started to pick up the first few. No problem, these were small ones. They would fit easily in his brand new rucksack; his birthday present from Dad. The first one that went in was a small, round rock. Ilias immediately remembered why he had put it there. It was right after Grandma Flower had died. She was Mum's mum and had a beautiful garden. Holding this rock, he could still feel how angry he was, how he had yelled at his dad: "Why didn't you help her? What kind of doctor are you?" Dad didn't say anything. He did not get angry, but with sad eyes told Ilias to go to the mountain and look for a stone.

The second one he picked up was a bit bigger and had some sharp edges. He had gone to the mountain of his own accord, just after he heard Mum and Dad fight for the first time. And the third one he put there when he realized what the water might do to the wings of the angels.

Carefully he picked up the fourth. As he let it slide into his rucksack he could hear his mum cry, alone, in her bedroom. When he reached for the fifth rock, he heard his father refuse to take him fishing, as always. "I'm sorry son, this trip is just for me and my friends." That stone landed in the bag with a bang.

The sixth was for that evening with Ella.
Mum and Dad were yelling again, and Ella
had come up to his room. She was upset and
crying, but he did not know what to say.
So he brought her back to bed and waited
until she was asleep. The next morning,
before school began, he went to the
mountain for this stone.

His bag started to fill up quickly, and so did
his head. Ilias decided it was time to climb
up for the very first time. The path was
narrow with lots of thick, prickly bushes on
both sides. He knew he would have to watch
out, maybe the climb would keep him busy.

As he went up, the stones on his back
weighed heavier and heavier with every step.
He knew he wasn't allowed to throw one out,
he had to carry his load.

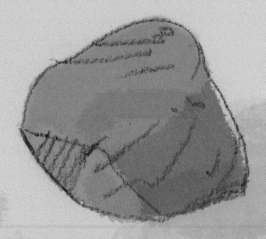

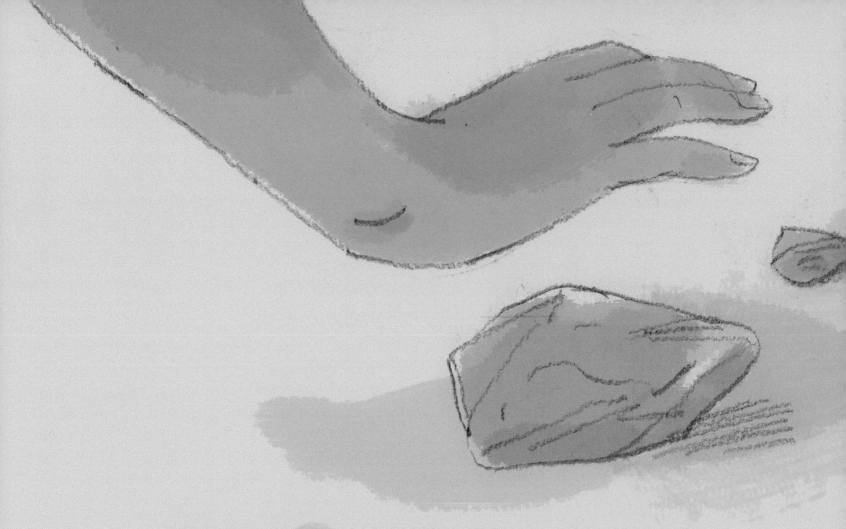

"That's what will make a man out of you,"
his father had said. And although Ilias had
no idea how or why, he did want to become
a man. Then he could be his father's friend or
even comfort his little sister. So he carried on
and did not even take a break to drink some
of the lemonade his mum had packed for him.

That day Ilias went up the mountain four times, almost to the top. He figured that if you had to do it, you might as well go all the way. Every time he kept his eyes straight on the path. He never stopped once to look at the waterfall, smile at a little squirrel or smell the beautiful, wild flowers. All he could see was the path he had to go, the stories in his head, and halfway up the mountain, two huge, angry piles where his mum and dad obviously had thrown down their stones.

When he decided to call it a day, he put down his last stone and stepped back. He heard his father's voice: "Everybody does it. They say it helps." Ilias did not know who 'they' were and he didn't think it helped at all. When he started he felt bad, and now he still felt bad. The only difference was that he could now add a sore head, a sore back and sore feet!

That evening his mum rubbed his back with lotion. "You will just have to keep doing it, dear," she said, "we all do". Ilias could feel her eyes wander out of his window, trying to find his father who was on his way to the mountain again.

"The fifth time this month," Ilias mumbled, but he was too tired to worry about it.

Chapter four
THE BAKER'S STORY

The next morning Ilias arrived at the bakery, early as ever. Today he would help out with the deliveries. "Hey Brownie." The baker welcomed him with a warm smile. "Good to see you, we have a busy day ahead!" Actually Ilias wanted badly to talk about his first trip up the mountain, but it was obvious that now wasn't a good time. Instead, he rode around all morning, delivering fresh French bread, pastries, plaited white bread for Sunday morning breakfast and one huge cake for the mayor's wife who would turn sixty tomorrow.

Nearly every customer gave him something extra and told him to say hello to his mum and dad. But nobody asked him about his first time alone up the mountain, though everyone knew he had just turned twelve.

When Ilias got back from his last delivery -
the huge birthday cake at the big red door
of the mayor's house - the baker was already
sitting outside with his feet dangling in the
cool water of the stream.

Ilias poured himself some lemonade and sat
down beside him. "Great weather, isn't it?"
the baker smiled. It seemed to Ilias he always
smiled. Or sang. Or was just being happy.

"Have you gone up the mountain often?" Ilias
tried to make it sound as casual as possible.
"Oh goodness me, yes, many, many times."
That answer shocked Ilias. Why would you
go if you were as happy as the baker?

"And you, what was it like for you?" the
baker asked, splashing his feet around.
He was the very first person who showed
any interest. Even his father had just given
him a small pat on the shoulder and said
something like "You'll get used to it." Then
they had dinner, Mum rubbed his sore back
with lotion and Dad went to the mountain.

"I did what I had to do," Ilias answered.
It was always so easy to talk to the baker.
"I took my rocks up the small path, all the
way to the top. I went up four times but then
my back started to hurt and I didn't want to
go anymore."

"Yes, but what did you think about it?" the baker asked again. Ilias stared at the water and sighed. "I didn't think anything." He sighed again. "I always thought I would feel something, but all I felt were my back and my feet. Mum said I had to keep doing it. I was thinking of going again today, maybe then..." His voice faded. He had no idea what 'then' could be.

The baker kept quiet for a moment. "You know what," he finally said, "I have to go up there myself this afternoon. If you help me first, I will help you later." Ilias had heard of people who carried their rocks up together, but nobody in his family did. His father probably wouldn't agree, but hey, what did he have to lose?

The baker went inside to change his clothes. He took his worn-out rucksack which already stood waiting by the door, and filled a smaller bag with some fresh buns and a bottle of lemonade. Then he kissed his wife. Just like that, right in the middle of the store, with all the customers watching and smiling. Ilias wished his father would kiss his mum like that for once.

The baker's wife waved them goodbye. "Have a good time! You too, Ilias!" Although he had no idea how time could be good carrying rocks up, he waved a cheerful 'Thank you!' and followed the singing baker. On their way to the mountains he thought about how different his life would be, if he was their son.

"Why don't you have any children?" Ilias asked, while he trudged behind the baker. Boy, it was hot today. The baker stopped and cleared his throat. "We have a son. But he is no longer with us."

"Why not?" Ilias could not believe that someone would not want to live with the baker, who suddenly picked up speed. Ilias had to work hard to keep up with him.

"His little heart wasn't strong enough for this world, he died when he was only six months old." He stopped suddenly, and Ilias nearly bumped into him. "Exactly nine and a half years ago. That's why I go up today." The baker started to walk again and so did Ilias - quiet as a mouse, though his head was spinning.

Why did that boy have to die? Was his father not able to cure him either? Just like with Grandma Flower? Why had his wife said 'have a good time'? Why, if the baker went up the mountain for a reason like that? Ilias didn't get it, but fortunately the air didn't get heavy like with his dad, and before he knew it the baker was already humming and singing again.

Chapter five

WALKING THE PATH

When they reached Ilias' mountain, the baker stopped. Ilias' face started to glow. He knew that every family made their own path, and had their own piles, but the mountains of course had to be shared. But he never knew he and the baker shared! It felt like a bond.

With a big smile on his face, he immediately wanted to go up, but the baker took his time. He clearly didn't want to pick up just any rock. He let several slide through his hands, but put them all carefully down again.
Ilias didn't say anything, afraid that he might stop the humming.

"This is the one," the baker finally said.
"Look Ilias, what a beautiful, beautiful rock!"
Ilias had never looked that closely at his rocks. He had just picked up a big one for a big sorrow, and a small one for when it was not too bad. But this rock was beautiful.
It was a bit flat, shiny white with a little grey and several tiny coloured lines going through.

The baker smiled, satisfied. "If you have to carry up a rock, it might as well be a beauty, don't you think?" Ilias agreed and decided to have a much closer look at his own rocks this afternoon.

When they went up the baker's path, Ilias
could not believe his eyes. Although it was
on the same mountain, it looked completely
different to his.

Here the sand was stamped with precision
and all the overhanging bushes were cut.
It almost felt as if the mountain had rolled
it down like a carpet to welcome him. Ilias
climbed without even so much as a scratch.

"If you have to walk the path, it might as well
be a nice one!" the baker said, while bending
forward to remove a small branch.

Halfway up they stopped at a small bench,
again a surprise. "I wish we had a bench!"
Ilias sighed longingly. The baker smiled and
handed him some bread and lemonade.
"I made it myself," he said, "and my wife
carved these." With his finger he followed the
letters A, T and E in the back, surrounded by
a heart. "The T stands for Thomas, that's me
of course and E stands for Esther, my wife."
His voice went soft. "And A, A is for Aram,
our son."

Ilias just took a big bite of his bread.
The bench, the letters, Aram, it was all a bit
much. Then the baker smiled again and took
a big bite as well. "Look," he said with his
mouth full, and he pointed his finger.

"There's my house. And there, right there is
yours. And there's the fountain. Can you see,
how beautiful the sun makes the water on the
angels' wings sparkle?"

Ilias hadn't noticed any of that yesterday.
He wondered if he had the same view.
Another thing on his checklist for
this afternoon!

When they moved on it only seemed a short trip up to the top. The baker told Ilias all about the trees, the flowers and some of the animals they came across and Ilias thought the day just couldn't get any better. He wanted to walk on like this forever, but suddenly the baker stopped. He put the rucksack down, took out the carefully chosen rock as well as a small shovel and a rubber hammer.

"If you have to place a rock, you might as well use the right tools!" The baker laughed out loud as he saw Ilias' face. He pointed his finger a few feet up the path. "There," he said, "right there."

Ilias looked up and saw the most amazing pile of stones he had ever seen. They were lying there, shining and sparkling in the sunlight as if they had just been polished. In between little plants peeked out with their soft little flowers dancing in the wind. These rocks were not just thrown down, no, they were carefully stacked like some sort of staircase.

"Let me show you the great spot I thought of for this special rock today", the baker said, ignoring the open mouth and big eyes of the face next to him.

Ilias carefully followed him up. With his mouth still a bit open, he put down his right foot on the first step. It felt surprisingly stable and firm! Above him, the baker went down on his knees and started digging a bit. Then he carefully put in the new stone and covered the edges firmly with a bit of sand so it would not move. "Higher and higher, Aram...," he whispered.

The whole experience confused Ilias so much that he had to sit down as well. But when he looked up, his last bit of breath was taken away by the view.

Not only could he see the whole village, but all the other mountaintops surrounding it as well. He saw little streams and waterfalls he didn't even know of! His eyes could follow the road, the one road out, right through the mountains. He saw his world like he had never seen it before, and the more he saw, the bigger he felt.

Chapter six

A DIFFERENT VIEW

The baker didn't seem to notice how confused Ilias was. Ilias could barely hear him still hammering a bit. But when he started to speak, his words entered Ilias' ears loud and clear: "You know, everyone has rocks to carry. When Aram died I was so mad... I took up so many stones... I threw them all on a pile and sometimes even one down again. But that didn't change a thing..." The hammering stopped.

"After a couple of months Esther and I decided to carry them up together. We didn't want separate piles anymore, you know, our grief was the same. Here at the top we both cried, even cursed and screamed sometimes. Nobody could hear us, only the mountain, and she didn't seem to mind. She became a friend who we visited often."

"One day, when I was really down, I took up the biggest rock ever and threw it down right on top of my pile. It made my body hurt as much as my heart, but when I looked up, I suddenly noticed I could see more than I ever did before... That was the day I decided to take all our rocks and start building these stairs. Now, for me it's not just about carrying the stones anymore, but what I can do with them. What they will make me see, what I may discover..."

Ilias just sat there, speechless. Finally, when
the baker sat down beside him, he felt brave
enough to ask the one question that went on
and on in his mind:
"Why didn't you tell my father about this?"

"I did," the baker softly answered. "But he didn't want to listen. You see, your father and I were good friends.

We always talked about how he wanted to take the road out, through the mountains, to see what lies behind. But then he met your mum, bought a house and had you and Ella. Although he loves all of you dearly, I could see he started to feel trapped. Losing Aram just made it worse. There was nothing he could have done, but he felt so bad, that he didn't know how to be my friend anymore. Later, when I told him about my stairs, and how far I could see without going anywhere, he just laughed at me. He isn't ready yet, Ilias. To change is never easy. To see things differently, to let go of the old ways, you have to be brave enough. Like you."

Ilias blushed, but deep down inside he knew it was true. He never just wanted to carry up rocks. He wanted to know why, and now he knew. It was a magical moment, and Ilias felt he could ask or say anything now. "Will you help me?" he whispered, afraid that his voice might break the spell.

"Of course, you helped me too." The baker also kept his voice down. Before Ilias could ask how, the baker continued, "I may not have my son with me anymore, but now I could show it to you. What's the use of discovering something if you can't share it?"

From that day on the villagers heard Ilias whistling or singing on his way to the mountain. It made them wonder, it made them talk. It made them shake their heads and tell each other that they always thought he was a weird kid, that he spent too much time with the baker, and that if he would have been their boy...

But Ilias wasn't. His mum and dad let him go. Sometimes still to pick up new rocks, but most of the time just figuring out the right place for the pile he already had.

With the bakers' help, he built a wall around a small garden that summer, just for Grandma Flower.

During Fall they worked on his own set of stairs. During Winter Ilias wasn't allowed to go up, because of the snow, but the stones he collected were the most beautiful ones he had ever seen.

Chapter seven
FINALLY

Before Ilias knew it, it was Spring again.

The melted snow from the mountains allowed
the small stream to run wild for a while.
When the fountain burst out its first splash
of water, Ilias was sure he saw the angels
show off their new wings. During last
Winter, the baker had started to complain
about the monument and, after a short
while, the villagers all agreed that it should
be restored. Mister Grissel, from GRISSEL'S
CHISELS & MASONRY and a good friend of the
baker picked out some perfect rocks at his
mountain and asked Ilias to help him.
He winked when he asked.
The happy kind.

On a beautiful sunny Sunday, Ilias was sitting in his room at his desk. His thirteenth birthday was coming up, and he had decided that it would be the perfect time to start his new, and best, mountain project ever - a watchtower! It was going to be a huge project, of course, and he concentrated on working out all the details.

Suddenly he heard footsteps coming up the stairs. He quickly hid the drawing of his new dream project, just in time. His father entered, a little uneasy - he hardly ever came up.

"It's a... see... your mum sent me", he said, holding the door with one hand. "She wanted to know, I mean... we want to know what you would like for your birthday."

Ilias' mind was now working at full speed. Was it the right time? What if it wasn't? But what if it was?

Then he closed his eyes, took a deep breath and said: "I want you to go up the mountain with me. I want to show you something." He could feel his father freeze.

He kept his eyes shut and pressed his lips together. He waited for the air to turn heavy, for his father to burst out, for the roof to come down.

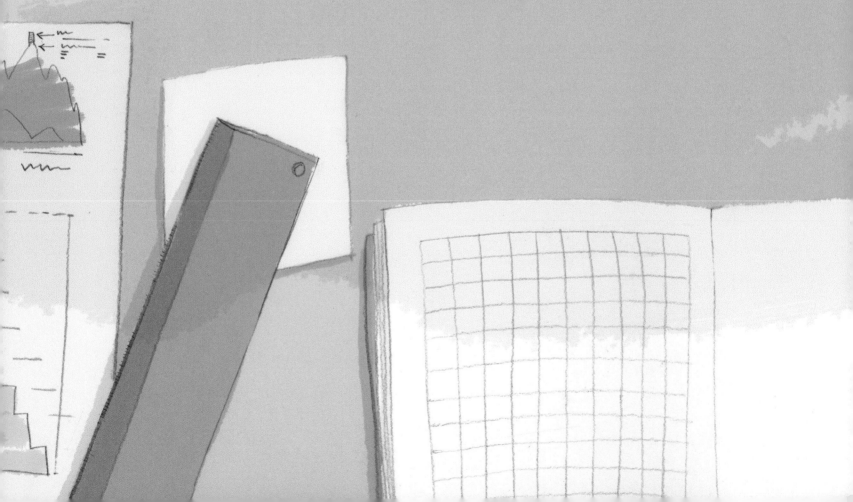

But none of that happened. What did happen,
was that he felt his father's hand stroke his
hair. He heard him say: "I'd love to come up
with you, Ilias. I would love to, son."
Then he quietly left the room.

A few minutes later, Ilias could still feel his
father's hand stroking his ordinary brown
hair. He felt tears coming out of his beautiful
brown eyes with the little spots of gold.
He had to blow his nose - which was a bit too
big, but quite common. He started to smile.
Yes, Ilias was a very ordinary boy.

But sometimes the most ordinary kids
do extraordinary things...

Lilian Kars, writer

"As long as I can remember, I express my
inner- and outerworld in stories.
Gazing out of the window of my study
I try to capture my experience in letters.
In simple words I try to cover Big Events,
so I and others may understand them
better. Some people call me a
writer, I prefer translater..."

Steffie Padmos, illustrator

"Steffie's passion is drawing the beauty
of flora and fauna of this world.
Besides creating picture books she also
works as a scientific illustrator, visualizing
biological and medical subjects.
Her creativity, interest for nature and
eye for detail strikes you when looking
at her work."